THIS CANDLEWICK BOOK BELONGS TO:

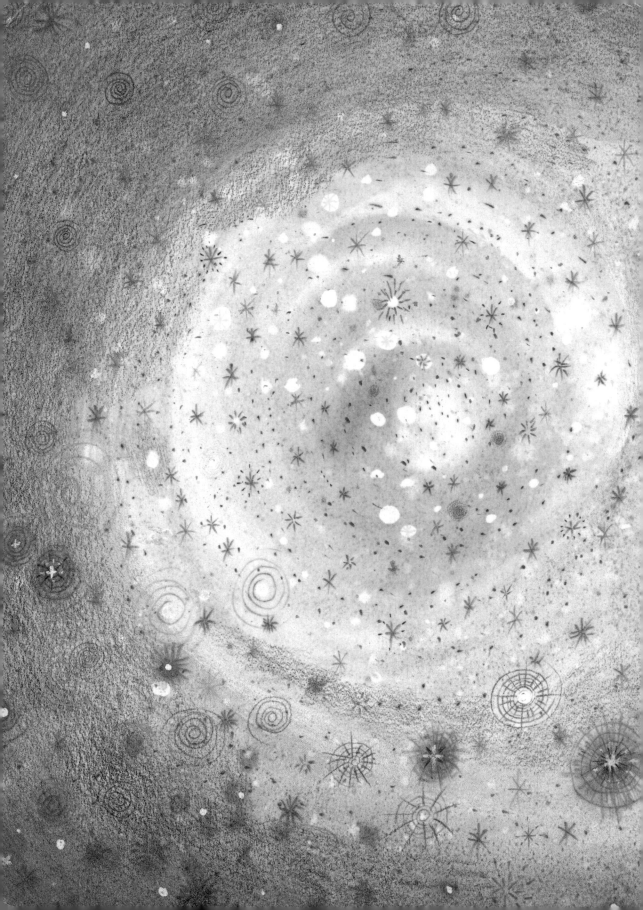

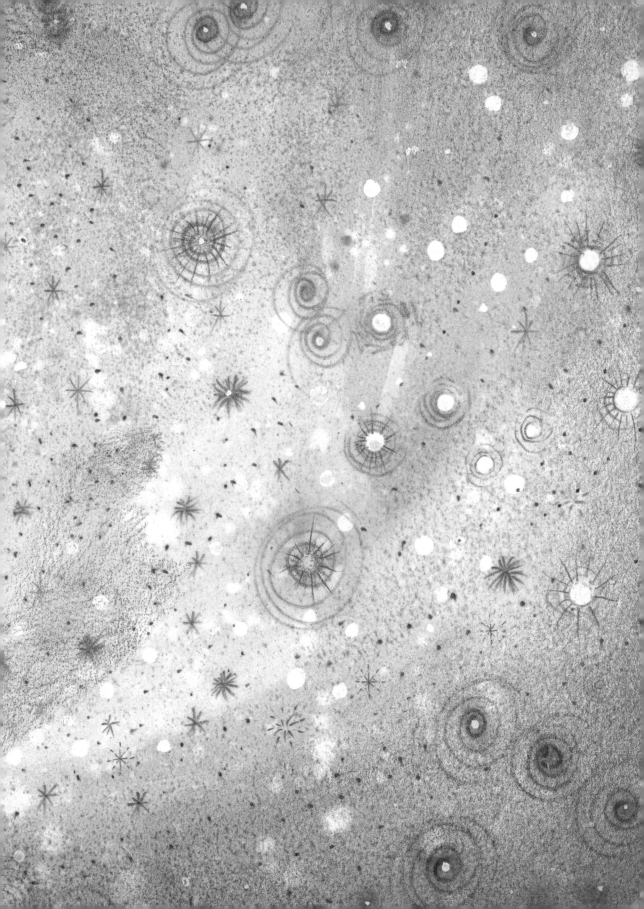

To Ninna and Oliver

First U.S. edition 2007

Library of Congress Cataloging-in-Publication Data is available.

Library of Congress Catalog Card Number pending

ISBN 978-0-7636-3571-8

2 4 6 8 10 9 7 5 3 1

Printed in China

This book was typeset in Optima.
The illustrations were done in colored pencil.

Candlewick Press
2067 Massachusetts Avenue
Cambridge, Massachusetts 02140

visit us at www.candlewick.com

Jane
and the
MAGICIAN

Martin Baynton

CANDLEWICK PRESS
CAMBRIDGE, MASSACHUSETTS

Jane was a knight. Not a pretend knight, but a fully qualified, highly trained Knight of the King's Guard.

One morning, Jane was polishing her armour when the dragon and the jester came by with royal news.

"We have been called to a meeting," said the jester.

"The Prince has got a royal cold," said the dragon, "and the King wants to cheer him up with a party."

"Where is my magician?" boomed the King.
"We can't have a party without magic tricks."

"He's gone," said Jane. "He couldn't make a rain
spell to water your flowers, so you sent him away."

"And now I want him back!" roared the King.

"We'll find him," cried the Captain of the Guard.

"We'll scour the land!" cheered the knights bravely.

"No," said the King, "you will stay and practise a
song for the party. Jane and her dragon will find our
missing magician."

Jane and the dragon searched all morning, but they could find no sign of the missing magician. Instead they found a problem – a wet and watery problem.

They found farmers floating in fields and cows climbing on cottages. They found babies in buckets and piglets in pots. They found turkeys in treetops and kittens in cups.

Jane and the dragon plucked them all from
the flood and set them down on top of a hill.

"What's going on?" yelled Jane.

The crowd pointed to a distant figure floating
on a cloud at the very centre of the storm.
It was the missing magician.

Jane and the dragon flew up to meet him.

"Look," laughed the magician, his eyes as dark as thunder, "my rain spell does work after all. I found the missing ingredient."

"What was it?" asked Jane.

The magician clapped his hands together.

"Anger!" he roared, and the thunder roared with him.

"Well done," shouted Jane. "But now you must stop."

"WHY?" roared the magician. "I've only just begun!" Again he clapped his hands and blue lightning sprang from his fingertips. It crackled across the sky and smacked into the dragon.

"No, no!" cried Jane, but it was too late. The dragon's wings folded like tissue-paper and he tumbled from the sky.

"Wake up!" cried Jane. But the dragon didn't
wake up. The thunderclap had closed his eyes
and closed his ears, and he hit the flood with a
terrible splash. Jane tried to keep his head above
the water, but it was impossible. She was sinking
herself, pulled down by the weight of her armour.

Down went Jane through the churning water.
Down and round, deeper and deeper.
She struggled to pull her armour off, but there
were too many buckles. So she drew her
sword and sliced through the leather straps.
Piece by piece her beautiful armour fell away
and she swam back to the surface.

Jane found her shield floating beside the dragon. She pushed it under his giant green head where it stayed afloat, bobbing on the water like a small raft.

When the magician saw what he had done, his anger vanished and the storm-clouds melted away. He went in search of Jane and the dragon and finally found them tangled in the branches of a tall tree.

"I'm sorry, Jane," he said quietly.

"Sorry is just a word," said Jane.

"A very short word," growled the dragon.

"You made this mess," said Jane. "If you're truly sorry, then you'll help to clean it up."

It took them the rest of the day, but with the dragon's hot breath to dry up the puddles and the magician's spells to repair the damage, the work was finally done.

When it was over, Jane pointed to one small rain-cloud which still hung above the magician.

"Can't you get rid of that one?" she asked.

"No," said the magician. "I'm still a little bit angry: I'm angry with myself."

Back at the palace, the party was not going well. The knights were singing their song and the Prince looked more miserable than ever. Then the Prince caught sight of the magician standing beneath his rain-cloud with the rain trickling down into his collar. And the Prince began to laugh. Then the King began to laugh, and so did the jester and the dragon and everyone else in the palace.

Finally even the magician began to laugh, and with a soft splutter his rain-cloud disappeared. In its place hung a bright and cheerful rainbow.

"Magic!" said Jane. And it was.

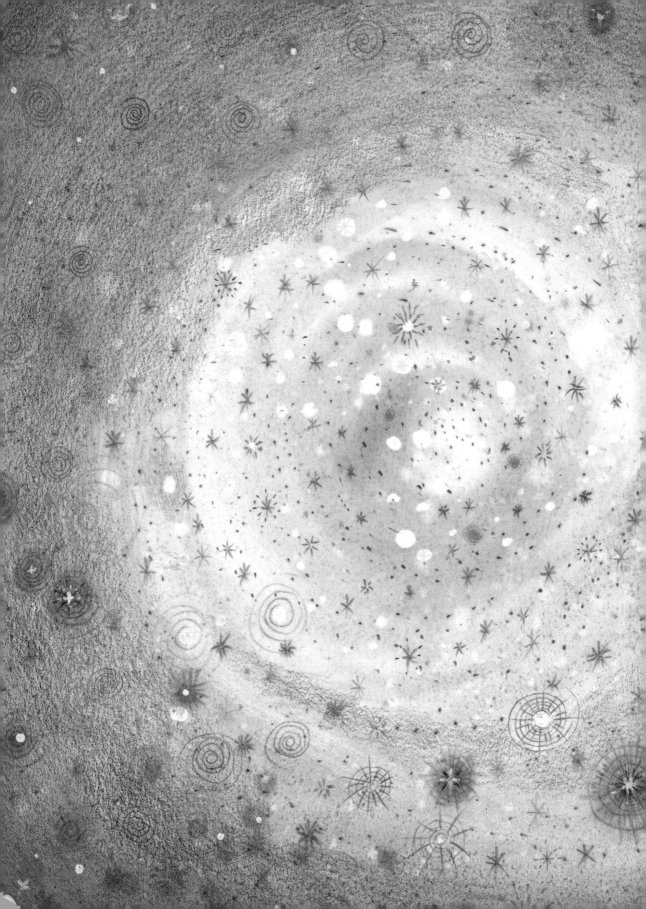

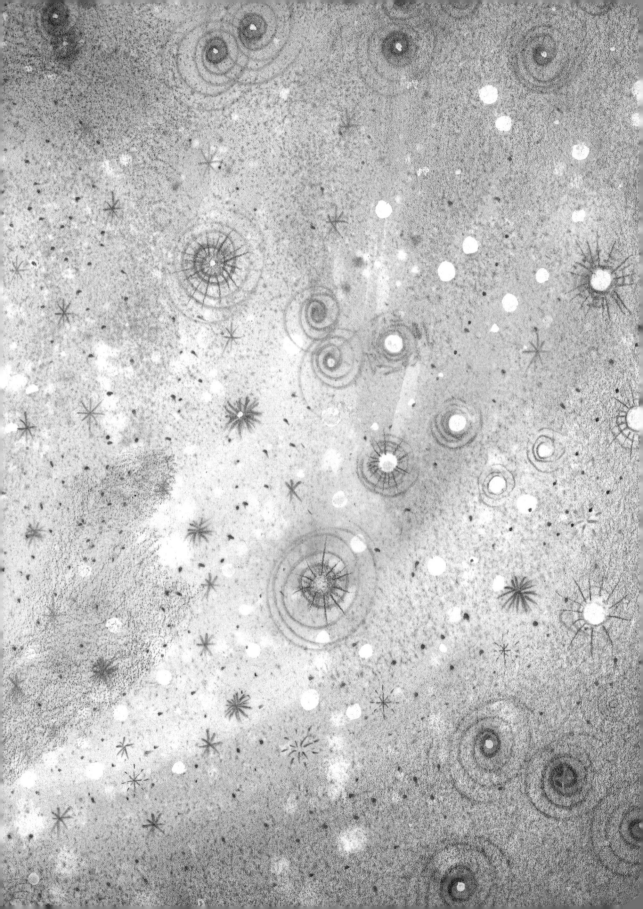

About the author...

Martin Baynton wanted to reverse the traditional treatment of fairytale heroines with this story. He says, "Fairy tales are tough on girls. Within their cruel pages, girls scrub floors, eat poisoned apples, sleep for centuries and are only saved when a handsome prince arrives to sweep them off their blistered knees into a world of Happily Ever After. Not so Jane. Jane saves herself and she most definitely does not want to live happily ever after. She wants adventure, danger, challenge – and 'happy' just isn't enough."

Martin has been a writer and illustrator since 1980 and has an international reputation for his books for children. He has recently partnered with the Academy award-winning Weta Workshop (The Lord of the Rings trilogy) and the Canadian children's television producers, Nelvana, to create a stunning animated television series based on the books, using the latest digital effects technology.

As well as writing and illustrating picture books for children, Martin also writes for the stage, television, film and radio. He was born in the UK and now lives in New Zealand.